Dean and Jean

by Liza Charlesworth

ISBN: 978-1-338-84445-0

Art Director: Tannaz Fassihi; Designer: Cynthia Ng; Illustrated by Michael Robertson
Copyright © Liza Charlesworth. All rights reserved. Published by Scholastic Inc.

3 4 5 6   68   26 25 24

Printed in Jiaxing, China. First printing, June 2022.

Meet Dean.
Meet Jean.
Jean is Dean's sis.

Jean is not mean.
But Jean did NOT
like to say "please."

"I need a seat!" said Jean.
"OK, sis," said Dean.

"I need a meal!" said Jean.
"OK, sis," said Dean.

5

Dean got Jean meat.

Dean got Jean
a big leaf.

6

Dean got Jean
a heap of peas.

Dean got Jean
a cup of tea.

Eat, eat, eat!
Jean is NOT neat.

"I need a tale!" said Jean.
"OK, sis," said Dean.

Dean got Jean *The Seal Who Did Not Say Please.* Read, read, read.

"I am rude like the seal in the tale," said Jean.

The Seal Who Did Not Say Please

"Can I PLEASE say
I am sorry?" said Jean.
"OK, sis," said Dean.

"Can I PLEASE get a
big hug?" said Jean.
"OK, sis," said Dean.
"It is a deal!"

13

Read & Review

Invite your learner to point to each *ea* word and read it aloud.

Dean

meal   peas

eat

Jean

seat   mean

deal

meat

seal

read

heap

I ♥ TREATS

neat

leaf

please

tea

15

Fun Fill-Ins

Read the sentences aloud, inviting your learner to complete them using the *ea* words in the box.

> tea please meal seal Dean

1. This story is about Jean and _____.

2. Jean said, "I need a _____!"

3. Dean gave Jean food and a cup of _____.

4. Dean read Jean a tale about a _____.

5. At the end, Jean DOES say "_____."